LAUGH YOUR S...

Jeremy STRONG

My Sister's Got a Spoon up her Nose!

Illustrated by Rowan Clifford

PUFFIN

This is for wonderful World Book Day Readers everywhere.

PUFFIN BOOKS

Published by the Penguin Group
Penguin Books Ltd, 80 Strand, London WC2R 0RL, England
Penguin Group (USA) Inc., 375 Hudson Street, New York, New York 10014, USA
Penguin Group (Canada), 90 Eglinton Avenue East, Suite 700, Toronto, Ontario, Canada M4P 2Y3
(a division of Pearson Penguin Canada Inc.)
Penguin Ireland, 25 St Stephen's Green, Dublin 2, Ireland (a division of Penguin Books Ltd)
Penguin Group (Australia), 250 Camberwell Road, Camberwell, Victoria 3124, Australia
(a division of Pearson Australia Group Pty Ltd)
Penguin Books India Pvt Ltd, 11 Community Centre, Panchsheel Park, New Delhi – 110 017, India
Penguin Group (NZ), 67 Apollo Drive, Mairangi Bay, Auckland 1310, New Zealand
(a division of Pearson New Zealand Ltd)
Penguin Books (South Africa) (Pty) Ltd, 24 Sturdee Avenue, Rosebank, Johannesburg 2196, South Africa

Penguin Books Ltd, Registered Offices: 80 Strand, London WC2R 0RL, England

penguin.com

Published 2007
1

Text copyright © Jeremy Strong, 2007
Illustrations copyright © Rowan Clifford, 2007
All rights reserved

The moral right of the author and illustrator has been asserted

Set in Baskerville MT
Made and printed in England by Clays Ltd, St Ives plc

British Library Cataloguing in Publication Data
A CIP catalogue record for this book is available from the British Library

ISBN: 978–0–141–32233–9

1. Emergency!

My sister's got a spoon up her nose. She has, honest! She stuck it up there herself. How daft can you get? Sometimes I think my whole family's daft – except for me, of course, and Mum. Mum says it's all Dad's fault.

'I didn't put it there!' he said.

'If you hadn't been showing everyone how to hang a spoon on the end of your nose it wouldn't have happened,' Mum answered.

'How was I to know Tomato would put the spoon *up* her nose instead of on it?'

Mum sighed. 'Her name is Rebecca, as you well know. Tomato is a silly name.'

'Maybe, but the back of a pizza van is a very silly place to give birth to twins. I think Cheese and Tomato suit the pair of them.'

'That's because you're an idiot,' said Mum. 'And I might remind you that it was your fault I gave birth to the twins in the back of a pizza van in the first place. If you'd got me to hospital in time it would never have happened. Now then, how are we going to get that spoon out?'

We looked at Tomato. She was sitting in her high chair, with a silly smile on her face and a plastic teaspoon hanging out of one nostril. She went cross-eyed trying to look at it.

'Poo!' she gurgled. Everything's poo as far as Tomato is concerned. It's her favourite word.

'Spoon,' corrected Mum.

'Spoo!'

'Close,' murmured Dad, while Tomato's twin brother Cheese picked up his spoon and began jabbing at his nose.

'No!' I said in alarm, snatching it from him.

'See what you've started?' demanded Mum.

Dad looked at me as if to say *Now what have I done?* I know how he feels. He does get the blame for quite a lot that happens in our house. There's a good reason for this. He often *is* to blame. But how could anyone know that Tomato would stick the spoon *up* her nose instead of *on* it?

Dad had been showing us the spoon trick. Can you do it? You hang a spoon from your nose by licking the spoony end and balancing it over your nose-tip. Even Mum had a go – until she noticed Tomato happily pushing her spoon in the wrong hole.

'We can't just pull it out,' she warned. 'It might do some damage.'

'Well, we can't leave it there either,' Dad said grimly. 'Suppose she grows up like that? Who'd want to marry a girl with a spoon sticking out of one nostril? I suppose if she's lucky she might find a boy with a spoon sticking up *his* nose.'

'Yes, and he'll be called Cheese. He's doing it again. Quick, Nicholas, get that spoon from your baby brother.'

It was true. Cheese was gaily trying to stick yet another teaspoon into his nose. It didn't fit so he started poking at his ear. I grabbed it just in time.

'What is it with this family?' asked Mum. 'Can't you do anything sensible? Just think for a few moments, would you? How can we get this spoon out? Ron, you remember when you couldn't get your ring off? We smeared washing-up liquid around it, and it slid off easily. I think washing-up liquid in a nose might sting though. We need something else that's slippery.'

'A fish?' suggested Dad. Mum fixed him with a steely glare.

'You want me to put a fish up Tomato's nose as well as a spoon?'

'It's something slippery,' Dad said, but I had a much better idea.

'Cooking oil?'

Mum shook her head again. Tomato gave a little cry. She was getting upset. We all were.

'Spoo,' whispered Tomato, with a tragic whimper. Cheese began crying too.

'Want spoon,' he said, waving both hands at me. 'Gimme spoon.'

'It's no good,' said Mum. 'I can't see how we're going to do this by ourselves. We'll have to take her to the hospital.'

We piled into the car and Dad drove us to Casualty. Cheese and Tomato grizzled most of the way and we got stuck in traffic. Dad opened his window and kept shouting 'dee-doo, dee-doo' at the top of his voice every time he thought we were going too slowly. When we finally reached the hospital Dad swept Tomato into his arms and bounded into the building.

'Emergency!' he shouted, plonking Tomato on the reception desk.

'Oh dear,' said the nurse. 'It's not difficult

to see what's wrong here.'

'Can you get the spoon out?' asked Dad anxiously.

'Oh yes, no problem. Let me take some details first. What's the baby's name?'

'Tomato.'

Mum sighed and elbowed Dad out of the way. 'Her name's Rebecca.'

'Her friends call her Tomato,' smiled Dad.

'Spoo,' murmured Tomato, gazing up at the nurse.

'Aren't you lovely?' cooed the nurse.

'Not with a spoon up her nose, she isn't,' Dad pointed out. 'Would you marry a girl like this?'

'Just ignore my husband,' said Mum. 'He's a very strange man.'

'That may be so,' agreed Dad. 'But I

am not nearly as strange as that man over there!'

Dad pointed to the corner of the waiting room. Guess who was there? Our neighbour, Mr Tugg. The one who does volcano impressions and explodes with anger every five minutes. Mr Tugg was standing there, reading a newspaper. He appeared to be completely jammed inside something long and thin. It jutted out in front of him and it poked out behind. He couldn't turn round in case he hit someone with it. He couldn't sit down because it got in the way of everything. All Mr Tugg could do was stand there and look a bit daft, because do you know what he had got himself stuck in? It was a long, metal stepladder. How on earth had he managed that?

2. The Competition

Mr Tugg was not the least bit pleased to see us when we went over to him. He hurriedly draped the newspaper over the front of the ladder, as if he was trying to hide it. No chance!

'Hello, Mr Tugg. We had to bring Rebecca in,' Mum told him. 'She put a spoon up her nose and we can't get it out, poor thing.'

'How about you, Mr Tugg?' said Dad. I could see that he was trying very hard not to stare at the ladder and laugh. 'Why are you here? Let me guess. Have you got a bad toe?'

Mr Tugg's eyes narrowed. He clearly thought Dad was winding him up, and he was right. Mr Tugg is very easy to wind up. Sometimes all you have to do is say 'good morning' to him and he gets angry. Mr Tugg started to explain.

'As you can –'

'Or have you got water on the knee, perhaps?' broke in Dad.

'As you can very well see for –'

'Or maybe it's something more serious – a banged head? Broken finger?'

'Stop interrupting will you?' roared Mr Tugg. 'As you can see I have got stuck in a ladder.'

Dad jumped back three paces. 'Oh, my goodness me,' he exclaimed. 'So you have. I didn't notice.'

'How did it happen?' asked Mum.

'First he fell off it, and then he fell through it,' said Mrs Tugg as she joined us. She had just returned with two cups of coffee from a machine. 'The silly man was working in the attic.'

'I am not a silly man,' snapped Mr Tugg.

'I think any man who wears a ladder round his waist is a bit silly,' said Mrs Tugg. 'As I was saying, he came down from the attic and his foot slipped. He grabbed the ladder sides and that made the ladder slip too. They would both have fallen to the floor but the top end of the ladder got stuck against a wardrobe and that was that.'

'I fell through the gap between the rungs,' Mr Tugg finished off, gritting his teeth. 'I've got grazed thighs,' he added, making it sound like he had the plague.

Mum and Dad looked at each other. 'Grazed thighs?' repeated Dad. 'Isn't that what we get from the Fried Chicken Takeaway?' Mum had to bite her lips to stop herself smiling.

'Mr Tugg?' a nurse called. 'Come this way please.'

'See you later,' Dad called after them as they made their way through to the treatment room. 'What a grapefruit,' he murmured.

'Don't you mean a lemon?' suggested Mum.

'No, I don't. Mr Tugg is too big a lemon to be a lemon so I reckon that makes him a grapefruit.'

'Hark who's talking,' Mum answered.

'Hey, look at this,' said Dad, picking up a leaflet and reading it aloud. '*Are you brave enough to take the Three Mile Challenge?'*

'What is it?' I asked.

'It's a charity event for the hospital – the Three Mile Challenge. You can sponsor someone to run a mile, swim a mile and jump a mile. JUMP a mile?! That's impossible.' Dad turned the leaflet over. 'Hey, good one. Guess what you do to jump a mile?'

I shrugged. 'Get fired from a cannon?'

'Good try,' said Dad. 'It's a parachute jump. You jump from over a mile high. Wow! I've always wanted to do that.'

'Since when?' asked Mum.

'Always, as in since now,' grinned Dad.

'Baby Tomato?' called the nurse, and everyone – EVERYONE – in the waiting room stopped nattering to each other and began gazing round to see who was mad enough to be called Baby Tomato. I've never seen Mum look quite so embarrassed!

She picked up Tomato and hastily made her way to the treatment room, while Dad and I stayed behind and played with Cheese. This usually means Cheese runs away as fast as he can and we have to catch him. It's very tiring, I can tell you. He's also pretty good at hiding, especially under people's coats and dresses.

Luckily it was not long before both Tomato and Mr Tugg came back. Mr Tugg was carrying his ladder cut into two pieces and Tomato was holding a lolly. The spoon had gone.

'She's fine,' said Mum, thanking the nurse. 'I don't know what we would have done if you hadn't been here,' she said gratefully.

'Yes, thank you,' mumbled Mr Tugg.

'Maybe you'd like to sponsor me in our charity event,' said the nurse quickly, snatching up a Three Mile Challenge leaflet. 'The money I raise will go the Children's Unit.'

Mr Tugg had a quick read. 'What a good idea. I'd be happy to sponsor you. How about you?' asked Mr Tugg, turning to Dad. 'Don't you think the hospital deserves our sponsorship?'

Dad saw this as a challenge. 'No, Mr Tugg. I am not going to sponsor a nurse.' He paused for a dramatic moment and then added: 'I am going to take part.'

'Take part?' repeated Mr Tugg, and his little moustache gave a violent twitch.

'Of course. I am going to run, swim and jump a mile, and all the money I get from sponsors will go to the hospital.'

'You're . . .' Mr Tugg broke off. I think he was going to tell Dad that he was mad, but he couldn't let Dad go one better than him.

'That's exactly what I was planning to do,' announced Mr Tugg. '*I* am going to run, swim and jump a mile too, and I'll tell you something right now, I shall beat you hollow!'

'Oh yes?'

'Oh yes!'

'Oh yes?' repeated Dad, raising himself on tiptoe to look even bigger.

'Oh yes!' cried Mr Tugg, standing on tiptoe too. They were nose to nose and they eyeballed each other.

I saw Mum look at Mrs Tugg and they rolled their eyes in despair. I don't know what they're worried about. It's going to be great! My dad and Mr Tugg in a running, swimming, jumping competition! I hope my dad wins.

3. The Wrong Person Goes Whoosh!

Dad's made me his trainer for the Three Mile Challenge! I've been trying to get him to do sit-ups, but he says he prefers lie-downs. Then I got him doing star jumps but he soon gave up. He said moon jumps are better than star jumps.

'What are moon jumps?' I asked.

'I curl up into a tight ball and pretend I'm the moon and you jump over me.'

'But that doesn't give you any exercise,' I complained. Dad just shrugged.

'That's why I prefer them,' he said. He is so lazy!

'Dad, do you want Mr Tugg to beat you?'

'No.'

'In that case you have to do what I say. It's no good making me your trainer and then not doing what I tell you.'

'I know, Nick, but when I made you my trainer I didn't expect you to be so hard on me.'

I tried to narrow my eyes the way Mum does when she's angry and won't stand for any more nonsense. 'Go and get your running kit,' I said severely. 'We're going on a training run.'

'Slave driver,' muttered Dad, and he trailed upstairs to fetch his gear. In the meantime I got my bike out of the garage. It's got a milometer on the front wheel so I can tell how far I've gone.

'How long will it take?' asked Dad, as he sat on the bottom step and pulled on his trainers.

'If you walk fast a mile takes about fifteen minutes. We should be a lot quicker than that. Come on.'

Dad set off at such a cracking pace I had to put on a big spurt to catch up with him. 'Don't use up all your energy straight away,' I advised.

'I'm fine,' puffed Dad. 'I could go for miles like this.'

'One will be quite enough,' I pointed out. Then he stopped, and bent over. 'What's up?'

'I'm done for,' he panted. 'We must have done a mile by now.'

I looked at the milometer. 'Dad, you haven't even run a quarter of a mile yet.'

'What? Your milometer must be wrong,' he complained. 'It's not working properly.'

'Yes it is. Get up off the pavement and start running.'

'I can't!' he wailed.

'Yes you can. Pretend Mr Tugg is right behind you and he's about to overtake. Come on!'

Dad dragged himself to his feet and staggered along the road. I cycled alongside, shouting encouragement. 'Come on, you can do it!' Dad hauled himself painfully along until at last we had actually completed a whole mile. Dad sank to his knees and fell forward on to a grassy patch.

'I'm dead,' he announced. 'How long did it take?'

'Fourteen minutes. You may as well have walked! Fourteen minutes, Dad. That's pathetic. Mr Tugg is much faster.'

'How do you know?'

'Because a snail with one leg missing could do it faster than you.'

'Snails don't have legs,' argued Dad.

'They have a foot,' I argued back. 'It's much the same thing.'

'No, because legs are longer than feet and they have knees in the middle and stuff like that.'

'Dad?'

'What?'

'We're talking a load of rubbish, aren't we?'

'Yes. It's a lot better than running.' He grinned at me.

'Right,' I told him. 'We're going to run back home now, and I mean run. Get on your feet, come on, quickly now, one, two, one, two.'

We made it home in ten minutes. 'But

only because it was downhill,' I pointed out. 'It's pretty pathetic really.'

As Dad was leaning over the gate, in what he called the recovery position, Mr Tugg's front door opened and he stepped out. He was wearing a whiter than white T-shirt, so bright it almost blinded you. He had little white shorts, long white socks up to his knees and running shoes. He stood on the doorstep and went through a flurry of warm-up exercises while Dad and I watched in amazement. Then he marched down the front path, took up a position and . . . whooosh! He was off.

We stared after him but it wasn't long before he'd vanished from sight. I looked at Dad. He had turned almost as white as Mr Tugg's T-shirt. Very slowly a frown crept on to his face. The frown became a dark scowl.

'You know what?' Dad muttered. 'We are going to beat that jumped-up twit. He won't get away with it. I shall be the King of Speed. He won't see me for dust.'

'But, Dad, he can run. He can really run – didn't you see how fast he was?'

'I am going to beat him,' Dad insisted.

'How?'

'I have a plan.'

'OK. What is it?' I asked.

'I'm going to creep into his bedroom tonight and I'm going to unscrew his legs and put them in the dustbin.'

'DAD!'

He gave me a crestfallen glance and wailed. 'He can run, Nick! He can run – properly. His legs go up and down and everything. He's bound to win.'

'No, he isn't. What you must do is train harder, and don't give up. Once you give up you have no chance of winning at all.'

'You sound just like my teachers at school when I was a boy,' groaned Dad, and I knew what he meant. I sounded just like my own teachers, let alone Dad's! However, the race was only a week away, so Dad was going to need a miracle if he was to have any chance of beating Mr Tugg.

'Come on,' I ordered. 'It's time for another training run.'

Dad groaned and struggled to his feet.

4. My Dad Has a Plan

Mum's been collecting sponsors for Dad's Three Mile Challenge. 'You're doing well,' she told him at breakfast this morning. 'You've raised almost three hundred pounds for the hospital so far.'

'Huh. I'd pay three hundred pounds not to take part. What is this stuff I'm eating? You've emptied the bird feeder into my cereal bowl, haven't you?'

Mum laughed. 'It's a power breakfast – all the things that will make your legs strong and give you energy. Just what a growing boy needs.' Mum winked at me, but Dad ignored being called a 'growing boy' and stirred his bowl furiously.

'I can't believe I'm doing this,' he said.

'You volunteered. It was your idea.'

Dad frowned. 'It's all your fault, Tomato. If you hadn't put that spoon up your nose I wouldn't be in this nightmare.' He picked at his food. 'These are rabbit pellets, aren't they?'

'They're raisins, as you know very well. Just eat up. Would it help if we played spoon planes?'

'Yes,' Dad grunted.

So Mum got a big dollop of cereal on his spoon and started from the other end of the kitchen. 'Here comes the plane, whizzing across the sky, open wide and in we fly!' Dad gulped down a planeload of breakfast.

'Good boy!' smiled Mum, patting Dad on the head.

'Cheese plane!' cried Cheese.

'Me plane!' yelled Tomato, banging her spoon on her feeder tray. Mum signalled me to help and it wasn't long before Mum and I were delivering food cargoes to two small babies and one very large one.

'Neeeyoowwwww!' went Mum, as Dad's spoon dived towards him.

'Neeeyowww!' I went, diving down on Cheese, who shut his mouth just as I got there. The spoon crash-landed on his chin, spilling food everywhere. Mum decided it was time to stop and be sensible, so Dad and I went out training.

He is getting faster. A bit. I don't think he'll be able to beat Mr Tugg though, and the race is tomorrow.

When we got back from our run this

afternoon Dad seemed a bit happier.

'I've got a plan,' he announced.

'Oh dear,' said Mum. 'Your plans always go wrong.'

'No, they don't. Not always. This plan is foolproof.'

'OK – what are you going to do?' asked Mum.

'I'm going to make some phone calls,' Dad told her. 'And the rest is secret. You will just have to wait and see.' Dad smiled and went upstairs to make his calls.

'What's your father up to, Nicholas?' asked Mum, but I didn't have a clue. 'Oh well, I guess we'll find out tomorrow,' she said eventually.

You'll never guess what Dad did for the race! The runners had gathered on the hospital car park, which was the starting point. There were all sorts there – fat, thin, young, old, men, women. Most of them were in running gear but a few had put on fancy dress. One woman was dressed as a fairy (a very big fairy), and there was an Egyptian mummy, a pirate and a fluffy purple penguin – at least I think it was meant to be a penguin. But there was no sign of Dad. He had left the house some time before us, saying that he needed to get ready, so it was worrying when we couldn't see him.

Mr Tugg saw us and he jogged across. 'Isn't your husband here, then?' he said to Mum with a little smirk. 'Chickened out, has he? Afraid I might beat him? I used to run for my school, you know.'

'Really? I used to run *from* mine,' Mum

murmured, but Mr Tugg ignored her.

'I was school cross-country champion, two years running.'

'Aren't your knees shiny, Mr Tugg?' observed Mum. And it was true. Mr Tugg's knees twinkled in the sun, almost as if he'd polished them for the race. My dad hasn't got twinkly knees. His are simply hairy, like a spider's.

'He's chickened out!' repeated Mr Tugg. 'I knew he couldn't take the competition.'

The starter bellowed some orders through her megaphone and the runners lined up at the tape.

'Where is he, Mum?' I asked anxiously.

'Nicholas, I have no idea what your father is playing at, but he'd better run because there is a lot of money at stake here – not to mention family pride.' A loud horn blared and the runners set off. Mum and I watched miserably while everyone went pelting off without Dad. Something must have happened to him, or he'd chickened out, just like Mr Tugg had said. It was horrible not knowing.

The race was circular, so the starting point was also the finishing line. Mum and I kept looking for Dad, but he was nowhere to be seen. I was desperately hoping he'd suddenly appear and go zooming after the others – after all, it wasn't too late to start until the race was actually over. But there was nothing.

'Here come the leaders,' Mum said gloomily. 'Mr Tugg's up near the front. I can tell by the moustache and sun flashing off his bald head, not to mention his knees.'

The winner crossed the line. It wasn't Mr Tugg, but he did come in fourth, waving both his arms triumphantly in the air. He came straight across to us, panting.

'Oh dear,' he smirked. 'Sorry your husband wasn't here.'

We were silent. We watched the stragglers arrive at the finish – mostly the ones who had dressed up in silly costumes and then discovered how hard it was to run in a race if you're covered in bandages, or you're a purple penguin. How ridiculous! In fact the purple penguin was last and it came slopping towards us on big flappy feet.

'Hello, Mr Tugg,' said the penguin in a very familiar voice. 'Were you looking for me?'

It was Dad. We should have guessed. Mr Tugg stepped back as Dad lifted off his furry head. He was sweating furiously. 'Phew, it's boiling in here. Of course, you can't run very fast, but it was good fun. Well done, Mr Tugg. You beat me.'

'I did, I did,' agreed Mr Tugg, proudly straightening up.

'Of course,' Dad went on, 'it was never a fair race – not with me dressed as a penguin.' He mopped his face and grinned. 'Not really a race at all, was it? Now, if only you'd come dressed as a penguin too . . .'

'Don't be ridiculous!' snorted Mr Tugg. 'I'll see you at the swimming. You won't be able to hide in your penguin costume then!' And he marched off. Dad looked at me and held out a hand.

'Gimme five!' he crowed.

5. Sink or Swim?

Dad seemed a bit low this morning. I thought he'd be sparking after his bit of fun with Mr Tugg yesterday.

'I didn't sleep well,' he complained. 'I kept having a dream about falling.'

'Are you worrying about the parachute jump?' Mum asked.

'No, of course not. Only a tiny bit.'

'Which tiny bit worries you?' Mum wanted to know.

Dad paused a moment. 'The jumping out of a plane bit.'

'Anything else?'

'And the falling bit.'

'Is that all?'

'And the landing bit.'

Mum poured his coffee. 'So, you're worried about the whole thing?'

'Yes,' admitted Dad. 'It's just a bit . . . scary,' he squeaked, and began chewing his nails.

'I know,' said Mum. 'When you said at the hospital that you'd do it, I did think you were being a bit, er . . .'

'. . . stupid?' suggested Dad.

'Brave,' smiled Mum. 'Heaven knows you're stupid enough most of the time. I think you're brave and I'm proud of you.'

'So am I,' I added.

'I wish you weren't proud of me,' Dad answered. 'If you two weren't so proud of me I could back out of it. I could tell the organizers I'm allergic to falling out of planes. But now you think I'm brave, so I shall have to do it.'

'And you can't let Mr Tugg go one better than you,' added Mum.

Dad gritted his teeth. 'No, that's true. I'm going to beat him at swimming and beat him at jumping.'

Mum put her arms round Dad. 'My hero!' she murmured. 'Try not to think about the jump. You've got the swimming first.'

'Yes, but that's easy. It's just up and down the swimming pool a few times.'

'Swimmy poo!' cried Tomato.

'Dad, it's thirty-two lengths.'

'Thirty poo!' Tomato gurgled.

'Thirty poo?' repeated Dad, stunned. 'But that'll take a week! Can I use a boat? I could borrow a pedalo from the lake in the park. Or maybe the Navy will lend me one of their submarines. I'd only need a small one.'

What is my dad like! By the time we set off for the pool Dad had gathered some bits and pieces he thought might help. All the other swimmers were there and none were in fancy dress this time. I suppose it's a bit difficult to swim in fancy dress, unless you go as a dolphin or a shark maybe.

Mr Tugg was there in his slinky racing trunks. He stood on the side and did some stretchy-bendy exercises. When he saw us he came straight over. 'Well, well, it's the penguin. I'm surprised you didn't keep your fancy dress on. You can't escape this time, I'm going to beat you hollow.'

'We'll see about that,' said Dad.

'I used to swim for my school,' snarled

Mr Tugg, 'when I wasn't running for it.'

'I'm off to get changed,' Dad said. 'I'll see you in the pool, Mr Tugg.'

Dad disappeared with his bag of gear. When he came back he was wearing his baggy, knee-length swimming trunks. He also had a face mask, a snorkel, extra-large flippers, a fat, red inflatable ring round his waist and armbands. Mr Tugg exploded.

'You can't wear that lot!' he shouted.

'Why not? Where in the rules does it say I can't wear all this? It's purely for safety.'

'I protest!' cried Mr Tugg and he called over the organizers. The organizers said that swimmers could wear whatever they wanted.

'It's the taking part and raising money that's important,' they added.

'But he's cheating! It shouldn't be allowed.'

'I shall welcome you at the finish line, Mr Tugg,' said Dad with a smile.

Mr Tugg jumped angrily into the pool, still protesting, and a few moments later the swimmers set off. My dad can't half splash about! He sent water every which way. It was like watching a whale trying to scratch itself. The other swimmers avoided him as much as possible. Meanwhile Mr Tugg demonstrated that his swimming technique was just as good as his running technique. He was making fast progress, but then so was Dad, thanks to his giant flippers.

I soon lost track of how many lengths either of them had done. In any case, it was getting a bit boring. The race seemed to go on forever, up and down, up and down. It was Mum who first noticed that

Mr Tugg was slowing down.

'He's not swimming as smoothly as he was at the beginning. He's splashing a bit more. Maybe he's tiring.'

It was true. Mr Tugg was splashing about a bit now. He was chucking almost as much water around as Dad.

In fact he'd come to a complete stop.

In fact he was sinking.

Mr Tugg was drowning! People began jumping to their feet and shouting for help. I saw the lifeguard race to the side. She was about to dive in when Mr Tugg suddenly rose to the surface again and took a great gasp of air. Someone had already rescued him. My dad!

Dad was pulling off his inflatable ring and pushing it under Mr Tugg. Then he yanked off his armbands and handed them over too. Finally he grabbed Mr Tugg with one arm under his chin and pulled him backwards to the side of the pool. Several people helped them both out of the water.

'Just don't ask me to give him the Kiss of Life,' he told the admiring crowd. 'Someone else can do that bit.'

Dad made sure Mr Tugg was going to be all right, then slipped back into the water and finished his mile. When he reached the end everyone cheered. I was so proud!

Afterwards, Mr Tugg came over to thank Dad for helping him. 'I overdid it a bit. I was trying too hard. Mind you, if you hadn't made me so angry at the beginning it wouldn't have happened. Never mind. You saved me. Thank you. That means we're even, so it's down to the mile jump.'

'I suppose you were the school's

parachute jump champion too?' said Dad.

'No,' answered Mr Tugg. 'Never done it before in my life.'

'Nor me,' Dad replied.

'I'll see you there tomorrow then,' said Mr Tugg.

'See you there,' echoed Dad.

'And may the best man win,' Mr Tugg threw back over his shoulder as he walked away.

It was a good thing he was walking away, because he couldn't see Dad's face. I've never seen him looking so scared in all my life.

6. How to Flatten the Lawn

Dad's been rehearsing for the parachute jump. 'When you land you have to roll over, Nick,' he told me as he pulled a rucksack on to his back.

'What's the rucksack for?' I asked.

'It's a pretend parachute. I've put some bath towels in there to bulk it up so it's more like a parachute pack.'

'That's clever, Dad – except that when you land the parachute won't still be packed. Hopefully it will have opened up and let you float down. Mind you, if the parachute doesn't open you will certainly be the first to reach the ground.'

'Ha ha, very funny, Nick, I don't think. How can you joke about these things?' He began pulling bath towels out of the rucksack. 'They wouldn't make very good parachutes anyhow,' he grumbled.

'But if it's raining when you make the jump, you could dry yourself with a towel on the way down.'

'I don't think you're taking this seriously,' suggested Dad with a scowl.

'Just trying to be useful,' I said cheerfully.

'Well, don't. Try and be useless instead.' He climbed on to one of the dining chairs, crouched down and held his nose. 'One, two . . .'

'Why are you holding your nose? You've done the swimming already.'

Dad reddened. 'Stop picking on me!

Let me concentrate.' He crouched down again. 'One, two, three!'

Dad leaped into the air, head-butted the ceiling by mistake, fell to the floor clutching his head, rolled over and crashed into the table. Mum came hurtling into the room to see what all the noise was about.

'What on earth is going on?' she demanded, as Dad tried to untangle himself from several table legs. He rubbed the top of his head.

'My parachute didn't open,' he complained.

'Dad was practising parachute landings,' I explained.

'Well, go outside and practise, if you must. The twins have just gone to sleep. You'll wake them up making that row.'

Dad took the chair outside and carried

on trying out his jumps and rolls. He had made about five jumps when he was stopped by a voice from next door.

'What are you doing?' asked Mr Tugg.

'There's a big lump on our lawn and I'm trying to flatten it,' said Dad.

'No, you're not. You're trying out parachute landings.'

'If you think that's what I'm doing why did you bother to ask?' snapped Dad.

'Because you're wasting your time. When you land you can't roll over.'

'Oh, really? You're an expert, are you? An expert who's never done a parachute jump in his life.'

'That's true. I haven't, but Mrs Tugg has.'

Dad's jaw dropped. The idea of Mrs Tugg on the end of a parachute was a bit funny. Mrs Tugg is a large lady and rather wobbly. Mr Tugg ignored Dad's splutters and went on.

'You see, first of all you don't roll over when you land because if you did you'd get tangled up in all the parachute lines and you could get dragged for miles by the wind.'

'I know that,' said Dad, who obviously didn't.

'And secondly,' Mr Tugg continued smugly, 'you couldn't possibly roll over anyway because you'll be strapped to someone else.'

This was news to Dad. 'Strapped to someone else? What do you mean?'

'You don't think they will let you make a first jump on your own? From that height? Oh no – you'll be strapped to an instructor and he'll guide you down.'

'I know that,' Dad repeated.

'Why did you ask, then?'

'Because I wanted to see if you knew,' Dad retorted. 'It was a test.'

Mr Tugg shook his head sadly, smiled to himself and walked off, leaving Dad seething. Dad looked across at me.

'What do you think, Nick? Do you think Mr Tugg is telling the truth?'

I nodded. Mr Tugg always told the truth. He was not the sort of person who made things up. After all, there was someone else on our street who did that almost all the time.

Dad shouted after Mr Tugg, who was just disappearing back into his house. 'I told you – I'm flattening this big lump!' And he threw himself on to the grass again. 'There,' he muttered to me. 'You can't even see it any more.'

Dad is definitely getting more and more nervous about the jump. He keeps asking me hard questions like, how fast does a body fall when it falls from a great height, and if he's strapped to someone else would he fall twice as fast? And, if the parachute doesn't open, would he be able to glide to somewhere he could land softly, like a haystack, a lake or a bed factory?

I pointed out that if Dad *was* strapped to someone else he wouldn't be able to glide at all.

'Can't you think of anything more helpful to tell me?' Dad answered.

'The instructor is certain to have a reserve 'chute,' I said, and he brightened a bit after that. He was even more cheerful when he noticed a small red spot on one arm. 'I might be getting chicken pox,' he told me. 'There's no way they'll let me jump if I've got chicken pox. Tomorrow morning I could be covered from head to toe in spots.'

7. Some Big Surprises

I don't believe it! Dad's covered in spots this morning! He *has* got chicken pox. Even Dad looks surprised.

'Don't go near Cheese and Tomato,' Mum ordered. 'We don't want them going down with the pox as well.'

'Pox!' repeated Cheese.

'Poo pox!' cried Tomato, lifting her cereal bowl and tipping it over her head.

'Oh, for heaven's sake!' said Mum. 'Nicholas, look after Cheese will you, while I clean up Tomato.' She glanced at Dad. 'Are you well enough to wipe down the table and Tomato's high chair, while

I sort her out?'

Dad nodded. 'I don't feel as bad as I look,' he said, holding up his arms and gazing at the spots. 'You do the twins and I'll do the washing-up and clearing. Then I think I'd better go and lie down for a bit.'

I played with Cheese in the room next door. I was a bit fed up actually. I had really been looking forward to the parachute jump and now Dad wouldn't be able to take part. Mum looked a bit dejected too when she came back from sorting Tomato. She went to see how Dad was doing.

'Have you got a temperature?' she asked him.

'I think so.'

'We'd better get you to a doctor.'

'I don't need a doctor,' said Dad. 'It's obviously chicken pox.' He took his hands out of the washing-up bowl and showed Mum.

'Are you sure?' asked Mum, studying his arms. 'I thought you had more spots than that. You had spots on your hands, didn't you?'

Dad was turning red. 'No, only my arms.'

'They were on the back of your hands when you showed me before – before you started doing the washing-up and your hands got wet. Let me take a closer look.'

Dad began to back away but Mum grabbed his arm. She took a wet cloth and rubbed at his skin.

'Oh, look,' said Mum. 'Fancy that. The spots have gone. I wonder why that is? It looks as if someone used a red felt-tip pen to make pretend spots on their arm. I wonder who that might have been?'

Now Dad was even redder than his spots. 'I think Cheese must have come and done it to me while I was asleep.'

'That is the most feeble excuse I have ever heard, Ron. Go and get yourself cleaned up. You've got a parachute jump to make this afternoon.'

'Must I?' squeaked Dad.

'What are you? Man or mouse?' Mum demanded.

'More like a squirrel, I think,' answered Dad.

'No – much more like a chicken, especially with those spots,' Mum shot back. 'Go and wash.' She rounded on me. 'And you can stop grinning like that, Nicholas. It's not funny.'

The only thing was, even as Mum said

this she winked at me – she just didn't want Dad to know she thought it was funny. Parents – honestly!

Dad got cleaned up and a little later we set off for the airfield. It was miles away and seemed to be in the middle of nowhere. There were a few small planes parked against the perimeter fence. Dad drove across to a huddle of huts and we got out of the car. A strong smell of frying bacon came from a small canteen.

'I'm going to get a bacon sandwich,' said Mum. 'Anyone else want one?'

'Yes, please!' I shouted.

Dad was as pale as anything. 'Not hungry,' he whispered.

'Look, isn't that Mr Tugg's car?' asked Mum, and I nodded. 'I can see Mrs Tugg getting out but Mr Tugg is still inside. I wonder why.'

Mrs Tugg gazed round the airfield, caught sight of us and waved. She came across. 'He won't get out yet,' she said. 'He's as white as . . .' Mrs Tugg looked at my dad, gave a quiet chuckle and leaned closer to Mum so she could whisper. 'Actually, my husband is about the same colour as yours! I've never seen him so nervous and scared.'

The two of them went into a huddle and carried on whispering and smiling and nodding at each other for a while. At last Mrs Tugg set off back to the car.

'What did she want?' asked Dad.

'She's just been telling me how scared Mr Tugg is. You wouldn't believe it, would you? Mr Tugg is scared!'

The change that came over my dad

was astonishing. He straightened his back, tipped up his chin and puffed out his chest. He even managed a grim smile, sort of.

'Huh!' chortled Dad. 'Of course he's scared! What a fool. Fancy being scared of a silly old plane ride and a silly old parachute jump. Ha! I'm going to go and have a word with the old scaredy cat.'

And with that, Dad marched off towards the Tuggs' car. He was halfway there when the driver's door opened and out stepped Mr Tugg himself. He started off towards my father. Mum grabbed my shoulder. 'Quick! I want to hear what they're saying, Nicholas. Creep a bit closer.'

We went and crouched round the corner of a building, just out of sight, but we caught every word.

'You're scared, aren't you?' Dad said

accusingly, and Mr Tugg snorted.

'Pah! Me? You must be joking. You're the one that's scared. Look at you. You're trembling from head to foot.'

'That's because there's a cold wind blowing,' my dad shot back. 'Besides, your face is as white as a bowl of rice, and a good deal soggier.'

'And you're gritting your teeth to stop them chattering,' snapped Mr Tugg.

'So you're going up in the plane then?' asked Dad.

'Of course. Why? Have you decided to stay on the ground?'

'No. I'm going up,' said Dad, gazing skyward. 'Right up there.' He gulped. 'Higher than the birds.'

Mr Tugg followed Dad's gaze. I saw him gulp as well. 'Me too,' he announced.

'Of course, if you decide to stay down here, then there won't be much point in me going up there.'

'Oh, I'm going up there all right,' said Dad, 'unless of course you say you're going to stay down here.'

'No, I'm going up,' said Mr Tugg.

'So am I!' cried Dad.

'So that's decided then!' said Mr Tugg.

'Yes, it is!' shouted Dad.

'Come on then. We'd better go and get kitted up. You lead the way.'

'No, after you,' said Dad. In the end they marched off side by side and disappeared into the kitting-out room.

Mrs Tugg came back and joined us. Mum looked at her and they burst out laughing. 'Worked like a dream,' said Mrs Tugg.

'What does she mean?' I asked Mum.

'Mrs Tugg and I agreed that I would tell Dad that Mr Tugg is scared – which he is. And Mrs Tugg would tell Mr Tugg your dad is scared – which he is. And neither of them would want to be outdone by the other, so they'd both egg each other on to go up in the plane. And it's worked – look.'

At that moment Dad and Mr Tugg reappeared. They were wearing full-length zip flying suits and harnesses. Their instructors came out with them. All four of them stood in front of us while Mum and Mrs Tugg took photos. Dad and Mr Tugg turned pale as they heard an aeroplane's engines burst into life.

'Time we got on the plane,' said the pilot. He turned to me. 'You coming as well?' he asked.

I was gobsmacked. What did he mean? I couldn't answer, I was so confused. 'Come on,' he repeated. 'There's room for a small one inside – unless, of course, you don't want to?'

'No! I mean, yes! Fantastic!' I glanced at Mum.

'Go on then,' she said. 'Hurry up or you'll miss the plane.'

I raced after them.

8. I Can Fly! (And So Can Dad)

I've been flying! I flew the plane! I did! I was allowed to go into the cockpit. I've never seen so many dials and instruments. The pilot let me sit next to him and I could see everything. It was like I was an eagle! The pilot was called Nick and we had a silly conversation.

> HIM: 'Hi, I'm Nick.'
>
> ME: 'Oh, you're Nick too!'
>
> HIM: 'I don't want to be Nick Two, I want be Nick One.'
>
> ME: 'Are you nicking my name?'
>
> HIM: 'You nicked my Nick first.'
>
> ME: 'I'm not a name nicker!'

HIM:	'I'll tell you what, just call me Fred.'
ME:	'Hi, Fred.'
HIM:	'Hello, Nick.'

Anyhow, Fred (Nick Two – or maybe One), was trying to drink a plastic cup of coffee while he was flying and that sort of thing is quite difficult. He was struggling with the controls and his coffee and you'll never guess what he said next.

'See that stick in front of you? Grab that and hold on to it while I drink my coffee. Just hold it steady. That's all you have to do.'

I took hold of the stick. I could feel it vibrating in my hand.

'Right,' said Fred. 'Keep her steady, that's fine. You're now flying the plane. Well done, captain.'

I couldn't help shouting back to Dad. 'I'm flying the plane, Dad!'

'You're what?! If I wasn't scared before I certainly am now!' Dad replied.

'Are you saying you're scared?' asked Mr Tugg but Dad didn't answer.

Fred leaned across and whispered in my ear. 'Those two are petrified! People usually are on their first jump. OK, I've finished my coffee. I'm taking back control now. Go and sit with your dad and then you can watch him make his jump.' I made my way back to the others. The two instructors were clipping themselves to Dad and Mr Tugg, standing at the edge of an open doorway with nothing but sky outside, over a mile above the ground.

Mr Tugg tapped Dad's arm. 'Maybe you're braver than me. I'm a bit scared.'

Dad turned and looked at him.

'You're scared?' he repeated, and Mr Tugg gave a curt nod. 'I'm terrified,' Dad admitted.

'We don't have to do this,' said Mr Tugg.

'Let's go home,' said Dad.

They looked at each other again and then stared out into the blue void. 'I don't want to die,' they both said at the same time.

'GO!' yelled the instructors and suddenly they'd gone. They'd jumped! Well, actually it was more like they'd been pushed! All I heard after that was a double scream.

'AAAAAAAAAAARRRRRRRRR RRGGGGGGGGHHHHHHHHHHH!'

It was caught by the howling wind and snatched away. I looked out over the edge.

Far back behind us I spotted two dark dots plummeting towards Earth. There was a puff of colour and out came the 'chutes. I let out a sigh of relief. The plane wheeled round and we headed back to the airfield.

Dad was already on the ground when we landed. He was standing next to Mr Tugg. They had their arms round each other's shoulders and they were both grinning like crazy while Mum and Mrs Tugg took photos of them.

'We did it!' they yelled. 'It was fantastic! We're going to do it again!'

'So who won?' I asked.

'What do you mean?'

'Who landed first? I thought you were having a race.'

'I don't know,' said Dad. 'I landed over there.'

'And I landed over there,' said Mr Tugg, pointing in the opposite direction. 'I don't know who landed first.'

They looked at each other and grinned again. 'It was a tie,' they chorused. Mrs Tugg and Mum and I shook our heads. We couldn't believe what we were looking at. Mr Tugg and my dad were friends. Weird! I wondered how long it would last.

All the way back home Dad could not stop talking about the jump. He was so excited and proud of himself.

'I can't believe I did it!'

'Well done,' said Mum.

'I can't believe I was scared!'

'You've been very brave,' said Mum.

'I jumped from over a mile high!'

'Yes,' said Mum, clenching her jaw.

'It was totally brilliant!'

'Yes,' said Mum, her jaw tightening even more.

'It takes a lot of guts to do a jump like that,' said Dad.

'Oh, for heaven's sake, Ron! You jumped from a plane! Yippee! And I've given birth to three children, two of them in one session. You want scary? You want bravery? Go and have your own twins!'

Dad looked at her in surprise. 'But I can't have babies. I'm a man.' Mum concentrated on driving and didn't answer for a while. Then she suggested that we stopped talking about parachute jumps and babies, so I sat in the back quietly and told Cheese and Tomato how I flew the plane.

'Plane,' repeated Cheese. 'Open mouth!'

'It was a proper plane,' I said. 'We

weren't playing spoon planes.'

'Poo plane,' gurgled Tomato.

'The mind boggles,' muttered Dad. 'I wish she'd stop saying "poo" all the time.'

'She'll grow out of it,' said Mum. 'And soon she'll be talking properly.'

'That's what I'm afraid of,' Dad grunted. 'Then there'll be two women in the house arguing with me all the time.' Mum didn't answer, but I could tell by the way she held her head that she was smiling.

It had seemed like a long day. I suppose that was because it had been so exciting.

Dad, Cheese and Tomato all fell asleep on the way home. Mum said it was like having three babies to look after.

'Sometimes,' she whispered to me as she drove, 'sometimes I think that you and I are the only sensible people in our family.'

When we got home there was a lot of sorting out to do, mostly Cheese and Tomato, of course. They needed feeding and bathing and changing before they got ready for bed. Looking after twins is a lot of work. I don't know how anyone manages with triplets, and quadruplets must be a nightmare. Anyhow, after their bath the twins played for a bit, until Cheese disappeared – again.

I went on a Cheese hunt and eventually found him sitting under the kitchen table, trying to get the top off the tomato ketchup. I was just congratulating myself on saving everyone from a ketchup catastrophe when I heard a muffled whimper from next door, where Tomato had been playing with her bricks. I hurried back to see if she was OK. Oh dear – she wasn't. She'd had a minor accident of the sticky kind. I picked her up and took her through to Dad in the other room. He was buried in the newspaper.

'Dad, Tomato's got a bit of a problem.'

'Really? What's the matter? She's not hurt, is she?'

'No, she's OK, sort of. It's just that . . .'

'What?'

'Um, well, she's got her potty stuck on her head and I can't get it off.'

The newspaper crashed down into Dad's lap. 'What is wrong with you lot? You know, sometimes I think I'm the only sensible person in this family.'

Mum and I burst out laughing. We couldn't help it. Dad's eyes widened. 'What?' he asked. 'What's so funny?' But we couldn't tell him. He rose from his chair with a sigh and peered up inside the yellow potty. 'Anybody in?'

'Pottymato,' said a sad voice from deep inside.

'You're telling me,' said Dad. 'You're definitely a pottymato, the pottiest Tomato I know. Come on, you lot, into the car. Guess where we're going?'

Ask Jeremy

Of all the books you have written, which one is your favourite?

I loved writing both **KRAZY KOW SAVES THE WORLD – WELL, ALMOST** and **STUFF**, my first book for teenagers. Both these made me laugh out loud while I was writing and I was pleased with the overall result in each case. I also love writing the stories about Nicholas and his daft family – **MY DAD, MY MUM, MY BROTHER** and so on.

If you couldn't be a writer what would you be?

Well, I'd be pretty fed up for a start, because writing was the one thing I knew I wanted to do from the age of nine onward. But if I DID have to do something else, I would love to be either an accomplished pianist or an artist of some sort. Music and art have played a big part in my whole life and I would love to be involved in them in some way.

What's the best thing about writing stories?

Oh dear – so many things to say here! Getting paid for making things up is pretty high on the list! It's also something you do on your own, inside your own head – nobody can interfere with that. The only boss you have is yourself. And you are creating something that nobody else has made before you. I also love making my readers laugh and want to read more and more.

Did you ever have a nightmare teacher?
(And who was your best ever?)

My nightmare at primary school was Mrs Chappell, long since dead. I knew her secret – she was not actually human. She was a Tyrannosaurus rex in disguise. She taught me for two years when I was in Y5 and Y6, and we didn't like each other at all. My best ever was when I was in Y3 and Y4. Her name was Miss Cox, and she was the one who first encouraged me to write stories. She was brilliant. Sadly, she is long dead too.

When you were a kid you used to play kiss-chase. Did you always do the chasing or did anyone ever chase you?!

I usually did the chasing, but when I got chased, I didn't bother to run very fast! Maybe I shouldn't admit to that! We didn't play kiss-chase at school – it was usually played during holidays. If we had tried playing it at school we would have been in serious trouble. Mind you, I seemed to spend most of my time in trouble of one sort or another, so maybe it wouldn't have mattered that much.

Want to keep laughing?

Enjoy even more hysterically funny adventures

from Jeremy Strong

Don't miss the side-splitting new escapade

from

Jeremy Strong

Nicholas's brother's bottom is so famous it's going on tour. The TV people are taking the family on the road – but somebody has to look after the goat!

And when the Bumper Dumper tour bus is kidnapped by giant babies it's up to Nicholas to save the day – can he get there in time?

Coming in April!